Santa's Birthday Gift

Sherrill S. Cannon

Eloquent Books

Eloquent Books
An imprint of Strategic Book Group
P.O. Box 333
Durham CT 06422
www.StrategicBookGroup.com

ISBN: 978-1-60860-824-9

Printed in the United States of America

Illustrations art, book cover art and book layout by
kalpart team - www.kalpart.com

For
Kelsey Beth,
who,
after I read her a story of the Nativity,
asked me...
"But where's Santa?"

Also for: Josh, Parker, Colby, Lindsay,
Tucker, Mikaila, Kylie, and Cristiano.

Special thanks to KJ and her team of illustrators
and book designers for the lovely illustrations
that enhance this book.

Thanks also to my daughters Kerry and Cailin for
their advice and support, to my husband Kim for
his patience and love, and to God
for inspiring this story.

In the small town of Bethlehem,
long, long ago,
On a night that was cold
and was starting to snow,

A woman named Mary
gave birth to a babe
And she wrapped Him in
swaddling clothes she had made.

She'd traveled a long way with
Joseph her spouse;
And finding no room
at an inn or a house,

They found a small stable
to help them stay warm
On that holy night, when
Baby Jesus was born.

She held Him and rocked Him
and gave Him her love,
For she knew that her baby was
sent from above;

And our Christ who would help
all the world to believe,
Was asleep in a manger
that first Christmas Eve.

And high up above,
there appeared a great light,
A glorious star
that lit up the night.

The light led the way
for three kings from afar,
They rode in on camels' backs
following that star.

These Wise Men knelt down
with the gifts they did bring:
Gold, myrrh, and frankincense,
fit for a king;

And lovely winged angels
filled up the sky,
Spreading the news
to the shepherds nearby,

And all came to see Him,
to tell of their joy
As they all clustered round Him,
this small, holy boy.

And far, far away,
at the North Pole that night,
An angel named Santa Claus
woke to starlight.

He saw that great star
and he started to smile,
For he knew that God's love
had been born as a child.

He was a toy maker;
he loved to make toys.
He made them all
for the good girls and boys.

He saw it was snowing,
so he hastened to pack
All the nice toys he had
in a large gunnysack.

He wore his red snowsuit
to help keep him warm
And with his toy sack,
he ran out to his barn.

He woke up his reindeer,
hitched them to his sleigh
And started out, letting the
star lead the way.

He traveled a long way,
then ran out of snow,
And wasn't sure how
he'd be able to go.

So he offered a prayer
as he looked to the sky
And suddenly his reindeer
were able to fly!

They flew through the air,
Santa Claus and his sleigh,
And arrived at the manger
where the holy Child lay.

And kneeling before Him,
with a sack full of toys,
He offered his heart
to this dearest of boys.

He leaned toward the Christ Child
and blew Him a kiss
And promised to Jesus
what would be his gift:

Each year on Christ's birthday,
he'd deliver his toys
To all children everywhere,
good girls and boys.

Then Santa saw all
the ones who were there,
Offering their praise and their
songs and their prayers;

The shepherds and animals,
angels and kings,
Each giving to Jesus
their most precious things.

He wanted to share with them
gifts he had brought
So he reached in his sack,
and he found quite a lot!

For he found that his sack
seemed to never grow empty,
No matter how much he gave,
there was still plenty!

For each toy he pulled out,
another appeared,
As his sack kept on filling up,
everyone cheered.

So he gave gifts to everyone,
and still finding more,
He went through the streets of town,
from door to door.

Then he jumped in his sleigh
and around the world flew,
With his sack full of presents
for me and for you.

So each year at Christmas,
Santa brings toys
To all good little girls
and all good little boys;

He remembers his promise
in a wonderful way,
He gives Christmas gifts
for the Christ Child's birthday.

CPSIA information can be obtained
at www.ICGtesting.com
Printed in the USA
LVIW011944171112

307650LV00002B